DiGuisto

The Switching Hour

The Switching
Hour

Adapted by Joanne Barkan
From the script by Marcy Gray Rubin
and David Adam Silverman

SCHOLASTIC INC.
New York Toronto London Auckland Sydney

Based on the TV series *Aaahh!!! Real Monsters*® created by
Klasky/Csupo Inc. as seen on Nickelodeon®

Cover illustration by Davis Henry
The text of this book was set in Stempel Garamond
The interior illustrations are from the video, enhanced in Adobe
Photoshop™ by Don Cassity

ISBN 0-590-18908-5

12 11 10 9 8 7 6 5 4 3 2   7 8 9/9 0 1 2/0

Printed in the U.S.A.   40

First Scholastic printing, October 1997

1

A jack-o'-lantern glowed in the
kitchen window at the back of
Nicky's house. It was early evening,
the day before Halloween.

Creeeeeak. The back door swung open.
Eight-year-old Nicky staggered out.

He was carrying four plastic garbage
bags stuffed with garbage. He lurched
down the porch steps and across the
shadowy backyard.

"Hey, Nicky-Wicky! You forgot
something!" shouted Jake, Nicky's
twelve-year-old brother. Jake leaned
out the door. He threw another
garbage bag across the yard.

Thwap! The bag hit Nicky and broke open. "Jake!" Nicky yelled. "I'm gonna tell Mom!"

Jake pretended to look scared. "Oooooh, I'm really shakin'," he said. He stepped back into the house and slammed the door.

"Brothers," Nicky muttered as he picked up the spilled garbage. He carried the bags to a covered metal can. He lifted the lid. He noticed something moving inside the can.

The *something* was purple with a wide mouth and huge floppy ears. It held an empty soup can in one hand. It stared at Nicky with round yellow eyes and burped.

"Aahhh!" Nicky screamed. "A monster!" He dropped the garbage bags and raced back to the house. "Mommy! Let me in!" he yelled, yanking the doorknob. The door was locked. "Let me in! There's a monster out here!"

Jake opened the door. He looked past Nicky into the backyard. "You mean *that*, pea-brain?"

Nicky turned around in time to see the silhouette of the long-eared creature. It streaked across the yard and disappeared behind some shrubs.

Jake held up two fingers. He wiggled them close to Nicky's face. "Nicky-Wicky, can you say *bunny rabbit*?"

Ickis wiggled his big floppy ears and shook his purple head.

"Ha! You shoulda' seen that kid run yesterday," he said. "He went screaming for his mommy. I scared him out of his wits. I'm baaaad. I'm real *baaaad!* I'm gonna scare a million kids tonight."

"Me, too," Krumm said, tossing his

eyeballs from one hand to the other. He brushed his long stiff armpit hair across Ickis's face. "I'm gonna make those kids wish they'd been born without noses!"

"You're the one to do it," Ickis said.

The two friends stood in a corridor of the elite Monster Academy. It was located beneath the city garbage dump.

Krumm pulled out a bag of dead beetles, ants, and horseflies. He popped a handful into his mouth and offered the bag to Ickis. "Trail mix?" he said.

Ickis was looking down the corridor. "Hey, there she is," he said. "There's Oblina."

Krumm belched as loud as he could to attract their friend's attention. Oblina's big red lips stretched into a huge smile. She hurried over.

"I can hardly stand it!" she said. "Tonight—our first Halloween as official student monsters! I am going to be marvelously horrific!"

Brinnnnng!

"That's the warning monster," Ickis said. "We have thirty seconds to get to class."

A hundred young monsters of every shape and color poured into the corridor. They rushed to the main lecture hall. Once inside, they quickly took their seats.

"I hear humans throw rotten eggs everywhere," Ickis whispered as he sat down.

Krumm drooled on the table. "Yum-m-m-m."

"Why waste a perfectly bad egg?" Oblina asked.

"Humans," Ickis muttered. "Go figure."

A tardy student scrambled for her seat. "Here comes the Gromble!" she hissed.

The room became silent. Footsteps rapped along the corridor. Then a large blue-green monster with long head wings and blood-red lips marched into the room. He glared at the class, tapping three of his four feet on the floor. The Gromble, headmaster of the academy, wore his usual black belt and red high-heeled shoes.

The Gromble smiled. "You all know, my dears, that tonight is your first Halloween. And we've been preparing for this glorious night all year."

The students nodded.

"It will be a night of mischief," the Gromble went on. "A night of mayhem. A night of *terror*!"

The students stood up and cheered.

The Gromble frowned. His voice became deep and threatening. "You also know that the results of last week's exam are in."

"Uh-oh," Ickis whispered. "I'm feeling queasy."

"You pus-mongers have really let me down this time," the Gromble shouted. "How hard could it be to scare the pants off an eight-year-old? *Out of an entire class, this was all you came up with?*"

The Gromble stepped behind his podium and pulled out a pair of pink pajama bottoms. A four-eyed monster in the front row giggled nervously.

"I'm glad you find this amusing!" the Gromble shrieked. "I suppose you and your classmates will enjoy a real laugh riot while you're sitting in your dorm rooms tonight!"

The students gasped.

"But, your Grombleness—" Four-eyes said.

"*Silence!*" the Gromble answered. "I have spoken. You ringworms are grounded. As far as you are concerned, *there's no such thing as Halloween!*"

"Halloween is a national holiday," Oblina whispered. "He cannot do this! Or . . . can he?"

The Gromble chuckled. "Just in case any of you is stupid enough to defy me, I'll have a guard at the academy exit." He pointed to the back row of seats. "Say hello to *the Snorch*."

Every eye in the room rotated in the same direction. The Snorch was dressed in a polka-dot robe and built like an overweight grisly bear. He bared his immense white fangs as he towered over the students.

Krumm moaned. "Not the Snorch again! Whatever happened to the honor system?"

The Gromble cooed sweetly. "Don't be afraid, my pets. The Snorch has been given strict orders not to hurt a hair on your noses."

The students all breathed a sigh of relief.

The Gromble shrieked with laughter. "He'll simply catch you and bring you to *me*!" He plucked a large green larva off the floor and dropped it delicately into his mouth. "After all," he murmured, "why should the Snorch have all the fun? What about *my* needs?"

2

The next evening, Nicky got dressed for Halloween in the bedroom he shared with Jake. He put on purple makeup, purple pants, a purple turtleneck, and purple slippers with upturned toes. He wore purple gloves and floppy ears.

Jake burst into the room. "Mom has just ruined my Halloween," he said.

"You can't go trick-or-treating?" Nicky asked.

"Worse," Jake said. "I gotta take you." He looked at Nicky's costume. "Adorable, dweeb. A purple bunny rabbit."

"I am not a rabbit," Nicky said. "I'm a monster—just like the one

10

I saw the other night."

"I don't care what you are," Jake said, grabbing one of Nicky's ears, "just follow orders."

"I'll be good," Nicky said. "I promise."

"Glad we understand each other," Jake said. He held out his hand. "Shake?"

Nicky grasped the outstretched hand. It fell off.

"Aaahh!" Nicky screeched at the top of his lungs.

Max, the family cat, leapt into the air. His fur stood on end. His green eyes gleamed.

"C'mon, dork," Jake said to Nicky. He picked up his rubber hand and stomped out of the room.

Meanwhile, at the academy . . .

"Sh-sh!" Oblina whispered. "Keep your voices down. You know the Gromble has spies."

Oblina, Krumm, and Ickis huddled in

11

a corner of the empty lecture hall. With them were two other students— Sparko and the Frunk. The room was dark, but the monsters were studying a detailed map of the dump. Sparko's orange eyes gave off just enough glow.

"The Gromble's not gonna ruin my Halloween," Sparko said. "The Frunk and I are slipping out through the main drainage pipe. If you guys wanna come, you can slide behind the Frunk."

The Frunk nodded. A stream of drool gushed out of each side of his mouth.

"Yeah, go with the flow," Krumm said.

Oblina shook her lips. "As appealing as that sounds, I think we will find our own way out."

"Well, actually I don't think I'll be able to go tonight," Ickis said. "I had some bad pencils for lunch. And wouldn't ya' know— they're sitting in my stomach like lead."

"Come on, Ickis," Oblina said. "Don't start."

Ickis's voice went up an octave. "But you heard what the Gromble said. He said if anyone —"

"Little Ickis could never, never disobey the big, bad Gromble," Sparko said.

"I could too!" Ickis retorted. "And I would — if I just didn't have this awful —"

"Ickis!" Oblina said. "Show some spunk."

Oblina, Ickis, and Krumm went back to their dorm room to plan their escape. A half hour later, they were slinking through a drainage pipe. It led to the academy's main entrance beside the garbage dump.

"Suppose we get lost," Ickis whispered, "or separated. Suppose it rains. My ears would fill up with water, and I'd drown. It could happen."

"Relax, Ickis," Oblina muttered.

Krumm was finishing up a sandwich—

slime on shoe leather. "I'd like some of those rotten eggs for dessert," he said.

Oblina clamped a tiny hand over Krumm's huge mouth. With the other hand, she pointed to the opening of the pipe just ahead. Ickis shivered.

The three friends peeked out of the opening. The Snorch stood about twenty feet away. Ickis clutched his stomach.

Oblina scanned the area, trying to think of a way past the Snorch. She noticed something.

"Psst!" she hissed, nudging Krumm. She pointed to a mound of sludge looming above the Snorch. An old toilet was perched on top of the mound.

Krumm chuckled softly. Taking aim with one eye, he threw his other eye at the toilet. It was a perfect throw. The toilet wobbled and fell. It crashed onto the Snorch's head, knocking him out cold.

The eye rolled back down the

mound to Krumm.

"Good shot, Krumm!" Oblina said. "Let us go."

Oblina dashed across the dump. Krumm ran after her. He stopped once and flipped a piece of watermelon rind into his mouth.

At the edge of the dump, Oblina turned around. She saw Ickis still standing in the opening of the air duct. She glared at him.

"I don't have a good feeling about this," Ickis muttered. "But—" He took a deep breath and raced past the Snorch.

Jake and Nicky stood on a street corner. Two of Jake's friends, Ted and Vic, walked up to them.

"Sorry, guys," Jake said. "I got stuck with the little turkey tonight."

Vic glanced at Nicky's costume. "Turkey? He looks like some kinda weird rabbit to me."

"I'm a monster!" Nicky protested.

"He actually thinks he saw one in our garbage can," Jake said. "Don't you, mush-brain?"

"Let's get going," Ted said. "I've got the ammo." He pointed to the ammunition belt on his military fatigues costume. It was packed with eggs.

"And look at this," Vic said. He held open his Navy pea jacket. It was lined with water pistols.

Jake adjusted the sword of his pirate costume and picked up a plastic bag. "I brought enough toilet paper to wipe up the entire neighborhood."

The three boys began marching down the street. Nicky hesitated for a moment and then followed them.

"This isn't Halloween," he muttered. "It's war."

Four blocks away, Oblina, Krumm, and Ickis hid behind some bushes near a red brick house. A boy dressed as a dragon and a girl dressed as a witch hurried up the walk leading to the house.

Krumm raised his arms high. "Like I told you," he said, "those kids are gonna wish they were born without noses. Watch this."

Oblina grabbed Krumm. "Wait, Krumm," she whispered. "We will go after them together."

The boy and girl stepped up to the front door of the house and rang the bell. A few seconds later, a woman opened the door.

"Trick or treat!" the kids shouted.

The woman smiled and held out a big bowl of pennies. The boy and girl each took a fistful and started back down the walk.

"Okay, ready . . . ," Oblina whispered, "set . . . go!"

The three monsters jumped out of the bushes. They blocked the sidewalk in front of the boy and girl.

"*Aaahh!*" Ickis shouted. He bared his teeth.

"*Aaahh!*" Oblina yelled. Her eyes and mouth opened to five times their usual size.

Krumm lunged forward, thrusting his armpits close to the kids' faces.

"Whew!" the boy said. "That's nasty!"

The girl reached out and scratched

one of Krumm's armpits. Then she bent in and sniffed. "A scratch-and-sniff costume," she said. "Awesome."

The boy looked at Oblina from top to bottom. Her eyes and mouth shrank down to their normal size.

"Hey, a transformer costume," the boy said. "Where'd you get it?"

The girl pulled one of Ickis's ears. "If it rains," she said, "they could fill up with water. You'd drown. It could happen, you know."

The boy and girl laughed.

"See ya around," the boy said as he turned to go.

"You can have these," the girl said to Ickis. She handed him all her pennies. Ickis popped some pennies in his mouth.

As soon as the kids were out of earshot, Oblina said, "They thought we were *humans* in costume!"

Ickis nodded. "How humiliating." He crunched down on one of the pennies.

"I've never been so embarrassed," Krumm said. He took a penny from Ickis and popped it into his mouth.

Oblina sighed. She nibbled on the edge of a coin.

"So, what do we do now?" Ickis asked. He took another penny.

"I could go for more of these copper-coated treats," Krumm said. He turned to the red brick house. "What did those kids say when the lady opened the door?"

"'Pick your meat,'" Oblina said.

"I think it was 'prick your feet,'" Ickis said.

"I definitely heard 'meat,'" Oblina replied.

"Let's try both," Krumm said. He smacked his lips and headed for the house.

Oblina and Ickis hurried after him. Krumm rang the doorbell. A few seconds later, the door swung open.

"Pr-pick your f-meat!" the monsters yelled.

The woman at the door stared at the three trick-or-treaters. Her mouth dropped open. "Oh, my," she said, taking a step back from Krumm. "You kids certainly are . . . the most . . . the most—" She turned and yelled, "Herb! Herb, you wanna get out here for a minute—please!"

A man came to the door. He was carrying a bowl of miniature candy bars. When he saw the monsters, his eyes opened wide. "Finally!" Herb said. "Some kids with imagination! I like it, Alice."

"But what are they supposed to be?" Alice asked.

"Well," Herb said, pointing to Oblina, "that one's a candy cane. And the purple one's like a jackrabbit or something. And the other one . . ." Herb sniffed and shook his head hard. "Whew! Son, whatever you are, you oughta take that costume off and get some air. I think you're starting to rot in there."

With his head turned to the side, Herb held out the bowl of candy. The monsters each grabbed a handful. Alice held out the bowl of pennics.

"Here, have some of these," she said. "*Quick.*" As she shut the door, she added, "Uh—nice job on the costumes."

Krumm popped one of the foil-wrapped candies into his mouth. "Hey, this is good, too. Especially the outside part."

The monsters quickly gobbled up all their pennies and candy.

"Let's get some more," Krumm said. He pressed the doorbell again.

"Pr-pick your f-meat!" the monsters yelled as soon as Alice opened the door.

She glared at them. "It was cute the first time, but don't push your luck." She shut the door.

"Cute?" Oblina said. "I hate cute. My

parents are not paying through the nose at the academy for me to be *cute*."

"Believe me, I know what you mean," Ickis said. "Cute is a major problem for me too."

"Cheer up," Krumm said. "We can always try pick-your-feeting at another house. More eats."

Oblina glanced up and down the block. "I suppose we could try that one," she said, pointing to a house across the street. It was decorated with ghosts and skeletons. "It looks a bit more inviting."

4

The monsters walked across the street and rang the doorbell of the decorated house. A teenaged boy opened the door.

"Pr-pick your f-meat!" the monsters shouted.

The boy yawned. "I think I'll die laughing," he said. "The party's in the den." He motioned the monsters to come in.

"This way," Oblina said, following the sound of children's voices.

The den was filled with eight- and nine-year-olds in costume. Some were playing pin the tail on the black cat.

Others were bobbing for apples in a large tub of water.

"Fun!" Ickis said when a girl dunked her head in the water. She came up with an apple in her mouth. Her face and hair were soaked.

Krumm took a close look at the apple. "What's the big deal?" he asked. "There aren't any worms in it."

"Hey, let's play the dead man's game," another girl said. "Get in a circle."

Everyone in the room formed a large circle. The girl turned out the lights.

"Now we pass around the grossest thing we can think of," she said. "I'll go first."

She stepped over to the refreshment table and grabbed a handful of gelatin dessert. "This is the belly fat of a decayed mongoose." She handed it to a boy in the circle.

"Gross!" the boy said.

He passed it to the girl standing next to him. She passed it to Krumm. Krumm tossed it into his mouth and swallowed.

"I've had better," he said.

A boy took some Silly Putty out of the pocket of his bullfighter's costume. "How about this? It's the booger of a *Tyrannosaurus rex.*"

The kids passed the putty around the circle. When it came to Krumm, he popped it into his mouth.

"M-m-m," he said. "Still chewy . . . after all these years." He swallowed the putty. "My turn now. I've got a good one—my very own eyes." Krumm handed them to the girl next to him. "Have a ball," he said.

"Are eyes supposed to be so slimy?" she asked. She passed the eyes on.

The lights went on. A woman stood in the doorway.

"What are you children playing in the dark?" she asked.

The boy holding Krumm's eyes looked at them. The black pupils grew bigger and then shrank.

"*Yiiiii!* These are *real!*" the boy screeched.

He tossed the eyes into the air and dashed to the door. Krumm dove to catch his eyes.

All the kids screamed and ran out of the room.

"What's the matter?" Krumm asked. "They're just eyeballs."

Ickis grinned. "Hey, we finally scared some humans."

"I say we do some follow-up," Oblina said. "Let us go!"

The three monsters raced from the den and chased the kids out of the house. The monsters caught up with the kids halfway down the street.

Just then, Nicky, Jake, and his friends came around the corner.

"Well, look at that!" Jake said. He quickly surveyed the group. "Major action straight ahead. Prime all weaponry. Attack!"

Jake, Vic, and Ted ran forward—water pistols, eggs, and toilet paper in hand.

Nicky began walking backward.

"I can't take any more of this," he muttered. He headed for a clump of trees in a large empty lot.

"Fire!" Ted shouted. He took aim and threw a rotten egg at the boy in the bullfighter's costume.

Krumm jumped in front of the boy and caught the egg in his mouth. Ted threw another egg. Krumm caught that one, too.

Jake and Vic were shooting water pistols and flinging toilet paper as hard and fast as they could.

Kids were screaming and running in all directions.

Oblina dodged the missiles and made it to the sidewalk. She crouched behind a mailbox.

Ted was firing off rotten eggs right and left. Krumm caught three more in his mouth. A fourth slammed into his nose and splattered.

Ickis looks
for a little
snack.

"Aaahh!
A monster!"
screams
Nicky.

The Gromble
strikes
fear in his
students.

A party...the perfect place for a scare.

Success!

"And what are we doing out after curfew?"

Meanwhile...
Ickis is
mistaken for
Nicky.

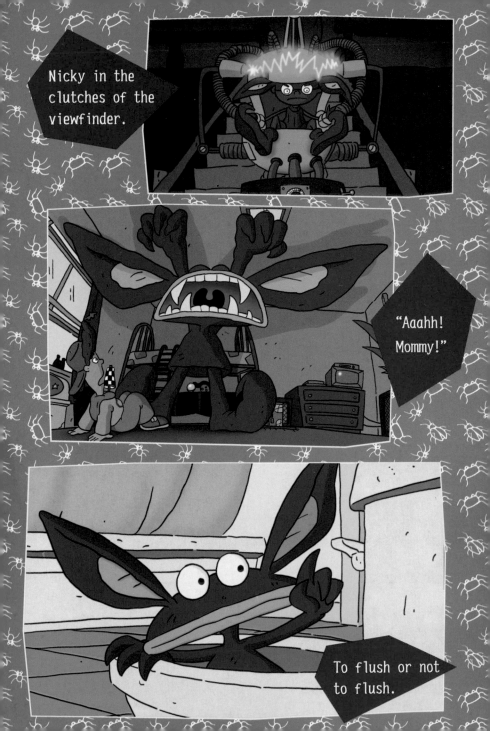

Nicky in the clutches of the viewfinder.

"Aaahh! Mommy!"

To flush or not to flush.

"That hurt!" he muttered. He scrambled to the sidewalk and joined Oblina behind the mailbox.

"Where is Ickis?" Oblina asked.

Krumm pointed to the middle of the street as he slurped up the splattered egg on his face.

"Let us get out of here," Oblina said. "To the trees, Krumm." She waved frantically to Ickis. "Follow us, Ickis!" she shouted.

Krumm and Oblina dodged the toilet paper, water, and shrieking kids as best they could. Krumm slowed down to lick some egg off the pavement. Oblina yanked his armpit hair.

"Will you please hurry!" she said.

Krumm and Oblina ran into the deep shadows around the trees. Krumm noticed a small purple figure with floppy ears.

"Ickis!" he said.

"How did you get here before us?" Oblina asked.

"I…I…" Nicky started to stammer.

Oblina interrupted him. "Those kids were vicious. What is the world coming to? I have half a mind to go back there and give them some of *this.*"

Oblina stretched her body straight up. Her eyes grew huge and bright green. Her mouth opened revealing gigantic jagged teeth. "*Aaahh!*"

Nicky staggered. He was trembling like a mound of Jell-O. He couldn't take his eyes off Oblina. He gasped and fell over flat on his face.

Oblina screamed. "Ickis has fainted!"

5

Krumm and Oblina bent over the little figure. They patted his cheeks and rubbed his ears, but he didn't respond.

Oblina sighed. "There is only one thing to do."

"Have a snack while we wait for him to come around?" Krumm asked.

"No, you idiot," Oblina said. "We have to carry Ickis back to the academy. You grab his feet. I will take his head."

Oblina and Krumm lifted Nicky up and began walking toward the dump. When they arrived, the Snorch was lying where they had left him. He was snoring loudly.

Krumm and Oblina took Nicky to their

dormitory room. They set him down on Krumm's bed under the old refrigerator canopy.

"Poor Ickis," Krumm said.

Oblina nodded. "Halloween is a major holiday. Perhaps we should have started him out on something easier—like Groundhog Day."

Oblina affectionately tickled one of Nicky's feet. His eyes popped open. He saw the two monsters leaning over him.

"Ohhh," he moaned. "I'm having one of those sick nightmares again."

Oblina gasped. "This is not Ickis. It's a *boy!*"

Krumm held one of his eyes over Nicky's face. "Hey, now that you mention it . . . " he mumbled.

"Uh-oh," Nicky said. "Something tells me this isn't a nightmare. It smells worse. Are you guys . . . real monsters?"

"Yup," Krumm said.

"*Help!*" Nicky shrieked. "Don't eat me!" He tried to jump off the bed. Oblina grabbed him.

"Calm down," she said. "We don't eat humans. Who knows where they've been?"

"Besides," Krumm added, "there'd be nobody left to scare."

"I suppose he's got a point," Nicky mumbled to himself.

"Now look here," Oblina said. "I am Oblina. This is Krumm. We demand to know what you have done with our friend Ickis."

Nicky looked puzzled.

"Well, did you see him?" Oblina asked. "Small chap, big ears, color of a fresh bruise . . . "

"Does he eat garbage?" Nicky asked.

Oblina nodded. "That's him."

"I've seen him in our big trash can," Nicky said. "I made my costume to look like him."

"Hm-m-m," Oblina murmured, "if you're here, that means—"

"It means my brother Jake's in big trouble," Nicky said. "Mom'll ground him for life."

"No, the important fact is that you and Ickis were switched," Oblina said. She began pacing up and down the room.

Krumm sat down on the edge of his bed with a large bag. "Trail mix," he said, offering Nicky the bag. "Share?"

Nicky peeked inside and shook his head.

Oblina stopped pacing. "Krumm," she said, "we must return this boy immediately and find Ickis." She grabbed Nicky's wrist and headed for the door.

Krumm threw a handful of trail mix into his mouth and followed Oblina. They all tiptoed along the dark corridor. When they got to a side exit, Oblina peered outside.

"All clear," she whispered.

"All clear?" a familiar voice said.

Krumm, Oblina, and Nicky whirled around. The Gromble stood at the end of the corridor glaring at them. He was wearing a terry cloth bathrobe.

"Well, well, well," the Gromble sang out. "And what are we doing out after curfew?"

"Ickis is sick," Krumm answered. "He needs some air."

"Right," Oblina added. "Nothing like a moonlit stroll by the disposable diapers to revive the spirits."

The Gromble frowned. "Ickis doesn't look ill to me. In fact . . . he looks more robust than usual."

"Your Grombleosity—" Oblina began politely.

"*Silence!*" the Gromble said. "Now get back into your room before I send *the Snorch* to tuck you in!"

6

Meanwhile, back on the street . . .

"Ouch!" Ickis yelled.

A smashed egg oozed down his neck. Ickis spun around and saw Ted winding up to heave another one. Before he could duck, Ickis felt someone grab both his ears. It was Jake.

"Oblina! Krumm!" Ickis called out. His words were lost in the ruckus.

Jake dragged Ickis away from the flying egg battle in the street.

"Nicky, you twit!" Jake shouted. He shook Ickis. "I told you to stay back. You could've gotten hurt. Mom would've grounded me for life."

"Uh . . . hold that thought, and I'll be right back," Ickis said. He twisted out of Jake's grasp and started running. Ted and Vic tackled him.

"I've had enough of you, Cottontail," Jake said. "It's a wrap."

Ted and Vic held Ickis down. Jake wrapped him from head to foot in toilet paper.

"Mommy's little bunny mummy," Jake said.

The boys pushed and dragged Ickis down the street for two blocks and to the door of a house.

"Hope we're not late for the party," Ted said. He rang the doorbell.

A minute later, Ickis stood in a corner of the basement. It was decorated with orange and black streamers and crowded with teenagers in costumes.

"So this is where they're keeping the toilet paper," said a girl dressed as a Gypsy. "Far out." She unwound a few feet of Ickis's wrapping and went into the bathroom.

Ickis stood next to the bathroom until he was completely unwrapped. Then he began moving slowly toward the door.

"Cool costume," a girl said. "Let's dance." She grabbed Ickis's hand and pulled him to the middle of the room. "You're kinda short," she whispered, "but you're a babe."

Jake walked up to them. "Sorry," he said to the girl. He grabbed Ickis by the back of the neck. "Romeo the rabbit has a curfew."

Jake kept a firm grip on Ickis and hurried home. His parents were watching television in the living room.

"Time for bed, Nicky," Jake's mother called out. "Tomorrow's a school day."

Jake pulled Ickis into the boys' bedroom and tossed him onto Nicky's bed.

"Sleep, dwarf," Jake said. He pointed

the tip of his pirate's sword at Ickis's belly.

"Sure thing," Ickis said to himself. "And the minute you leave, I'm outta here."

Ickis closed his eyes and pretended to sleep for a few seconds. The next thing he knew, light filled the room. Someone was shaking him.

"Get up, bonehead," Jake said. "Breakfast is ready. And you'd better get out of that costume before Mom sees you. Halloween is over, bunny boy."

As Jake turned to go, Ickis scrambled under the bed and crouched in the far corner.

"You know, Nicky," Jake said. "Sometimes your level of stupidity astounds me. Now come out!"

Ickis didn't move. Jake marched out of the room and was back almost immediately. He was carrying a broom.

"You asked for it, nerd," Jake said. "Broom handle for breakfast."

Jake thrust the broom handle under

the bed. He heard a loud *crunch!* followed by noisy chewing. He pulled the broom handle out. Half of it was gone.

"Mom!" Jake yelled. "Nicky broke the broom!"

Jake's mother appeared in the doorway. "Nicky, get dressed this minute. You don't want to miss the school bus."

Ickis crawled out from under the bed and walked toward the closet. Jake and his mother went into the kitchen.

Ickis peered inside the closet and pulled out Bermuda shorts and a Hawaiian shirt.

"Over my dead body," he muttered.

Ickis threw them on the floor and took out Nicky's good suit. "This is worse."

Finally he looked in the dirty laundry pile. He found a pair of baggy pants and a T-shirt. He sniffed them and sighed happily. "B.O. on polyester."

Two minutes later, Ickis climbed onto a kitchen chair. He was wearing the

T-shirt, pants, a pair of high tops, and a baseball cap pulled down over his ears and most of his face.

Jake's mother put a soft-boiled egg in an egg cup in front of Ickis. "Eat up," she said.

As soon as she turned back to the sink, Ickis put the egg and the cup in his mouth. He swallowed them whole and burped. He headed for the front door. Jake was waiting.

"You're such a dweeb," Jake said.

"Thanks," Ickis answered.

The school bus pulled up in front of the house. Jake yanked Ickis down the front walk and pushed him onto the bus.

7

Ickis glanced around Miss Bitiger's classroom and moaned softly. *This is the pits,* he thought. *I actually miss the Gromble!*

"Now, class," Miss Bitiger was saying, "yesterday we learned all about Wanda Frimler's penthouse condo with the wraparound terrace and sweeping river views. Today Nicky will tell us all about his house. Right, Nicky?" She motioned to Ickis to come to the front of the room.

"My house?" Ickis mumbled. He walked up the aisle between rows of desks. "Uh . . . let's see . . . " he said dreamily. "Well, it's got the best trash you'll ever find."

Several kids in the class chuckled.

Ickis went on. "There's enough maggots and chicken bones to feed a family for weeks." He didn't notice the growing laughter. "You can really smell the tuna cans. And when it rains, the mud and glop come up to your waist."

The students began cheering.

Ickis stood tall and proclaimed, "I live in a filthy, disgusting dump!"

Miss Bitiger grabbed Ickis by the T-shirt and pulled him out of the noisy room. "You know where you're going, young man," she said.

Ickis groaned. "The trash compactor?"

Miss Bitiger pointed to a sign that read, DETENTION ROOM. She pulled open the door and pushed Ickis inside.

A man sat at the front of the room, reading. He didn't look up when Ickis entered. He just pointed to one of the many desks.

Ickis sat down and glanced around at his

new classmates. One had spiked green hair. Another had a large serpent decal on each arm. Another wore immense combat boots.

"Hey, it's sort of homey in here," Ickis said.

"What are *you* in for?" one boy asked.

"Disrupting class," Ickis said.

"Naughty, naughty," the girl with the green hair said. "Like this?" She shook Ickis's desk wildly.

"Or like this?" the boy with combat boots asked. He fired a spitball at Ickis's face.

Ickis's eyes opened wide and began to turn red. "No, more like this," he said with a snarl. He leaned over and bit off one leg of the boy's chair. The boy crashed to the floor.

The green-haired girl winked at Ickis. "You're kinda short," she said, "but you're a babe."

Meanwhile, beneath the garbage dump, in another classroom . . .

"I hope you all had a most happy Halloween," the Gromble said to his students. He waited a second and then looked shocked and embarrassed. "Oh, I forgot—you missed all the fun. How terribly insensitive of me!"

Oblina rolled her eyes as the Gromble howled with laughter.

Nicky sat between Oblina and Krumm on one of the long benches. He still wore his Ickis costume. He glanced around nervously.

A monster with a face on each side of her rotating head sat nearby. She winked at Nicky.

"Hi, Ickis," she said. Her head rotated. An eye in her other face winked. Her head began to turn faster. Her eyes winked like blinking lights.

Nicky shivered. "Stay close to me," he whispered to Oblina and Krumm. Krumm sidled over and rubbed against him. "Whew!" Nicky said. "Not that close!"

"Silence!" the Gromble bellowed. "It's time to review last week's assignment." He snapped his fingers. "Bring in the viewfinder."

A four-legged monster wheeled in a contraption that looked like a chair with arms and a metal helmet. Wires and rods connected its various parts. It sat on a base with levers and dials.

"What is that?" Nicky whispered.

"The viewfinder records images from your brain. It projects them onto a big screen," Oblina said.

"Yeah, like home brain movies," Krumm added.

The four-legged monster pulled out a portable movie screen. The Gromble crossed his arms and surveyed the students.

"Who will start?" the Gromble asked. "Master Ickis, I think."

Nicky's eyes closed. He looked as though he might faint.

"With all due respect, your Grombleness," Oblina said, "Ickis has not been himself lately."

"*Nonsense!*" the Gromble yelled. He grabbed Nicky and pushed him onto the viewfinder's seat.

The Gromble flipped a switch. The helmet descended over Nicky's head. Clamps closed around his wrists. A green light flashed.

Everyone stared at the movie screen. An image flickered and then steadied.

"Here comes disaster," Oblina muttered.

On the screen, Nicky in his costume grasped an outstretched hand. The hand fell off. There was an ear-piercing screech. A black cat leapt high into the air. His fur stood on end. His green eyes gleamed.

As the picture faded, the students began to cheer and applaud.

"Definitely not shabby," Oblina said to Krumm.

The Gromble pulled Nicky out of the viewfinder. "Splendid, Ickis," he said. "Five point seven is your technical mark. Five point nine for artistry. And to think I said you'd never amount to anything."

The Gromble handed Nicky a large slug. Nicky looked at it and grimaced.

"Go ahead," the Gromble said. "Eat it."

Nicky swallowed hard and stammered, "I—I—"

Krumm snatched the slug. He swallowed it whole.

"Ickis is counting calories," Krumm explained.

"Thanks," Nicky whispered as he and Krumm took their seats.

The door to the lecture hall opened. The Snorch walked in. He had a large swelling on the top of his head. He spoke to the Gromble in a low grunt.

"This is not good," Oblina murmured.

The Gromble clenched his fists. He

glared at the class and snarled. "I now have reason to believe that some of you hangnailed little sneaks were out last night."

He walked slowly over to a row of students. He bent down and grabbed the monster with the revolving head. "Was it you?" he asked in a low voice.

"No, no, your Grombleness!" she squeaked. "I would never—" Her head spun around furiously.

The Gromble let go of the monster. He studied the students carefully, one by one.

"Oh, dear," Oblina whispered. "Apparently we were the only ones to go out last night."

"The Gromble's gonna bite our heads off for sure," Krumm answered.

Nicky turned to Oblina. "But you said monsters don't eat humans, right?"

"True," Oblina replied, "but I never said we don't eat other monsters."

"But what about me?" Nicky

asked. He looked frantic. "The Gromble thinks I'm Ickis."

"Pipe down," Oblina said. "If we do get out of this class in one piece, we'll take you right home."

"Oh, great," Nicky said. "*If* we get out ... "

"Quiet!" the Gromble roared. "Make no mistake. I will find out who disobeyed me, and when I do ... " Saliva oozed from his mouth. "Now get out of my sight!"

8

"Krumm, this is no time for snacking," Oblina said. "We are on a mission."

"I consider snacking my mission," Krumm muttered. He sighed deeply and dropped the rusty bedspring that he was munching. He hurried across the empty lot just behind Oblina and Nicky.

"Turn left here," Nicky said. "When we climb over that fence, we'll be in my backyard."

Once they were in the backyard, Nicky pointed to a side window.

"That's my bedroom," he whispered. Crouching low, they snuck along the side of the house. The window was open a few inches. Oblina stretched up to peek inside.

Ickis sat on a chair in baggy pants and a baseball cap. His hands and legs were bound with cord. Two older boys were sitting on a bed, dividing up a pile of candy.

"Whataya say, Vic," one boy said to the other. "Should we share this stuff with Nicky?"

"Yeah, Jake," Vic said. "Right after we give him a big hug. We're great baby-sitters."

The two boys laughed and continued dividing up the candy. Ickis squirmed.

"Poor Ickis," Oblina whispered.

"Got ants in your pants, Nicky?" Jake asked.

"I've got to go to the bathroom," Ickis said.

"Tough noogies," Jake answered.

Ickis shrugged. "Have it your own way. It's your chair."

Jake looked up. "I'd better untie the twit," he said. He got up and undid the cords. "Be back here in sixty seconds," he said, "or I'll flush you down the toilet myself."

"That's probably the best way of getting out of here," Ickis muttered.

Oblina bent down and whispered to Krumm and Nicky, "Ickis is going to try to get back to the dump through the sewer system."

"Fun but risky," Krumm said. "You could end up anywhere."

Oblina stretched up to the window again.

Ickis slid off the chair. Jake reached out and grabbed his baseball cap. Ickis's purple ears popped up.

"You have a serious wardrobe problem," Jake said. He yanked one of Ickis's ears hard. "I told you Halloween is over."

Ickis whirled around and tried to shove Jake. "Cut it out!" he said.

"Pipsqueak!" Jake yelled. "Prepare to die!"

Jake threw Ickis down on the floor and sat on top of him.

"I said—cut it out!" Ickis repeated.

"Uh-oh, here it comes," Jake said. "Time to cry for Mommy."

Jake pulled on Ickis's ears again. When they didn't come off, Jake shouted, "I'll teach you to use my super glue without asking." He raised his fist.

Ickis looked terrified for an instant. Then his eyes turned red. His head and body began to expand. He grew larger and larger and pushed Jake aside. He opened his huge mouth, revealing sharp fangs.

Vic jumped off the bed. "*Eeeeee!*" He ran out of the room screaming.

"Mommy!" Jake shrieked. He

dove under the bed.

Ickis shrank to his usual size and ran toward the bathroom.

"Let's go!" Oblina said.

Oblina pushed open the window. She gave Nicky and Krumm each a boost up to the sill. She climbed into the bedroom after them.

"Quick—to the bathroom," Oblina said.

She and Krumm burst into the bathroom. Ickis was standing in the toilet. He was about to flush it.

"Krumm! Oblina!" he said when he saw his friends.

"Oh, Ickis," Oblina said. "We really tried to get here sooner."

"Are you okay?" Krumm asked.

Ickis grinned. "I'm better than okay. I'm *baaaad!* Bad to the bone. You're lookin' at one real monster!"

"I knew you had it in you!" Oblina said. She gave Ickis a hug.

"Cheers!" Krumm said. He stuck his head into the toilet bowl and took a long drink.

The three friends went back to Nicky's bedroom.

"See ya around!" Krumm called to Nicky.

Nicky waved. Then he bent down and peered underneath the bed. "Oh, Jakey," he sang out.

"H-help!" Jake stammered. "M-m-m-monsters!"

Nicky wiggled two fingers under the bed. "Jakey-Wakey," he said, "can you say *bunny rabbit?*"

Oblina lowered herself out the window and helped her friends down. They climbed over the fence and hurried back to the dump.

"Listen," Ickis said as they slipped through the academy's back entrance.

"It's the all-academy assembly monster!" Oblina said.

"I don't like the sound of this," Krumm said.

Students filled the corridor. They were rushing to the lecture hall. Krumm, Oblina, and Ickis joined them.

When everyone was seated, the monster stopped ringing. The room was silent.

The door swung open. The Gromble stomped in. He stood in the center of the room and cracked his knuckles one by one.

"None of you puke-faces confessed to going above ground on Halloween," he said. "So I did a little detective work. I have my spies, you know."

"He'll never be able to pin this on us," Ickis whispered.

The Gromble continued. "With the aid of a rusty tweezer and a few other tools of persuasion, I found out everything."

"We're doomed," Ickis whispered.

"Oblina, Krumm, and Ickis would you please stand up?" the Gromble said.

The three friends rose. Ickis was trembling. Oblina was biting her huge lip. Krumm was bathed in sweat.

"Class," the Gromble said, "I want you all to look at these three. Take a good, long look, for they . . . "

"I'm going to throw up," Ickis said.

"Don't talk about food now," Krumm muttered.

The Gromble cleared his throat. "They are the leaders of tomorrow!"

"I told you not to sweat it," Krumm whispered.

Ickis beamed. "A leader of tomorrow!" he murmured.

The Gromble went on. "Unlike the rest of you slobbering ninnies, these students acted like real monsters. They went out on Halloween!"

Oblina's eyelashes fluttered. "Ah, yes, we are good."